THE BOOGIE WOOGIE MAN

SWEETWATER
PRESS

The Boogie Woogie Man

Copyright © 2008 Sweetwater Press

ISBN-13: 978-1-58173-761-5
ISBN-10: 1-58173-761-0

Printed in China

THE BOOGIE WOOGIE MAN

Meagan Sanders

SWEETWATER
PRESS

Little Sarah-Lou was four years old. She could write her whole name, go almost all the way across the monkey bars, and even color inside the lines. But Sarah had one itsy-bitsy, teeny-weeny problem. She was afraid of the Boogieman.

Every night at bedtime, Sarah would take extra long getting ready so she wouldn't have to go to bed. She sat in her bath and refused to get out until all the bubbles were gone. She brushed every tooth ten times and always pretended to need help getting her pajamas on.

"Everybody knows that the Boogieman won't come out until all mommies and daddies leave!" Sarah huffed one night, wiping tears from her eyes as her daddy peeked in her closet and under her bed for any sign of the monster.

"Nope, no Boogieman here," he said, kissing her forehead and turning out the light. "Sweet dreams!"

"Who can even dream with a Boogieman about to get them?" Sarah whimpered, looking around her dark room and then back at her closet.

Everything sure looked safe enough. And that's when she heard it.

BANG!

BOOM!

BOP BOP BOPPITY!

Just like many other nights, strange clattering started coming from inside her closet. Little Sarah was about to jump right off her bed and run to her mommy when CRASH!

Her closet door hurled open and something BIG, GREEN, and hairy came out.

"THE BOOGIEMAN!" screamed Sarah as she dove under her covers and closed her eyes.

That's when she noticed the unusual sounds filling up her room.

Dum Diddy Dum Diddy Da Da!

Was it...
Could it be...
music!?

Tap Tap Tapitty Tap Tap!

Sarah peeked out from under the covers. Sure enough, there in the middle of the room was THE BOOGIEMAN! He had glowing red eyes, sharp fangs, long yellow claws, and...

TAP SHOES?!

Sarah dropped her covers and stared in shock as she watched the Boogieman spin and twirl and tap all over her room.

"Are you… Aren't you the Boogieman?" she whispered to the whirling monster.

"Boogieman?" The big green beast asked, surprised. "I'm the Boogie Woogie Man! I'm the best boogie-er in all the closets on this street!"

A dancing Boogieman? Now, that didn't sound scary at all. And by that time, Sarah-Lou's foot had started tapping along with Boogie Woogie's zingy zangy music. Soon, they were wiggling and shaking and boogieing all around the room.

They boogied on the bed with a
BANG, BOOM, BUMPITY!
They boogied on the toy box with a
TRIP-TRAP, THUMPITY!

They boogied on the bookshelf, they boogied on the desk, they even boogied on the walls.

And before she knew it, little Sarah-Lou and big ol' Boogie Woogie were all boogied out and asleep on the rug.

When Sarah woke up the next morning, Boogie Woogie was gone. But from that night on, things were different at Sarah's house. She got out of the bath before even half of the bubbles were gone. She brushed her teeth just enough, and even put her pajamas on right the first time. And her daddy didn't need to check her closet anymore.

Her parents were so happy that little Sarah-Lou had gotten over her fear of the Boogieman, that they never even asked her why she rushed off to her bedroom each night. They never asked her why she wasn't afraid of the Boogieman anymore. And they never, ever asked her...

why she wore
tap shoes to bed!